ALSO BY DON FREEMAN

TILLY WITCH
CORDUROY
THE GUARD MOUSE
A RAINBOW OF MY OWN
DANDELION
THE TURTLE AND THE DOVE
SKI PUP
COME AGAIN, PELICAN
CYRANO THE CROW
SPACE WITCH
NORMAN THE DOORMAN
THE NIGHT THE LIGHTS WENT OUT
FLY HIGH, FLY LOW
MOP TOP
BEADY BEAR

By Lydia and Don Freeman
PET OF THE MET

HATTIE
THE BACKSTAGE BAT

STORY AND PICTURES

BY DON FREEMAN

THE VIKING PRESS   NEW YORK

To
Marjorie, Boris, Lisa, and Arthur

FIRST EDITION

Copyright © 1970 by Don Freeman
All rights reserved
First published in 1970 by The Viking Press, Inc.
625 Madison Avenue, New York, N.Y. 10022
Published simultaneously in Canada by
The Macmillan Company of Canada Limited
Trade 670–36253–0   VLB 670–36254–9
Library of Congress catalog card number: 72–123017
Printed in U.S.A.
Pic Bk

The backstage of a dark, empty theatre is a lonely place where only a bat would feel at home.

To a little bat named Hattie, this *was* home.

She had lived in the Lyceum Theatre all her life, so she had never seen a green tree or a haunted house. Nor, for that matter, had she ever flown in the bright moonlight the way other bats do.

Hattie's sky was the vast space high above the stage. Every night she flew about for hours at a time, swooping in and out among the ropes and rafters and between the stage curtains.

Then, when she was tired, she landed on her favorite perch, folded her wings tightly against her sides, and hung upside down by her tiny claws to sleep.

The only person who knew about Hattie was Mr. Collins, the stage doorman. He came in every morning to sweep the floor and to keep things neat and tidy.

There hadn't been a show in the old Lyceum Theatre for quite a long while, but Mr. Collins was never lonely. He had Hattie to keep him company.

Once he made her a tiny hat out of odds and ends he found in an old costume trunk.

Each noontime Mr. Collins pulled his chair to the middle of the stage and shared his lunch with his friend. He knew that bats like to nibble flowers even more than they like crumbs, so he always brought Hattie a daisy for her dessert.

While they ate Hattie listened as Mr. Collins chatted about the wonderful plays and shows that had been presented on this very stage.

One afternoon he had very important news to tell Hattie. "Starting today, some actors are coming here to rehearse a new play," he said seriously. "That means you will have to stay out of sight. I don't know why, but people get terribly frightened if they see a bat flying around."

Then, with his long-handled broom, Mr. Collins shooed Hattie into the rafters. "I'm sorry to have to do this, my dear," he shouted, "but it's for your own good as well as mine. We want the play to be a success, don't we?"

So Hattie did as she was told. The actors and actresses had no idea a bat was hanging high above them as they sat in a circle reading their scripts. Since this was a mystery play, they spoke their lines mostly in whispers.

Day after day, the actors came in and rehearsed their parts until they knew all their lines by heart. Day after day Hattie kept well out of sight.

It was only late at night that Hattie flew down to the stage and ate the tasty
tidbits Mr. Collins had left especially for her.

One morning Hattie awoke to the sound of hammering. The scenery for the play was being set up on the stage.

There below, Hattie saw, for the first time in her life, not only a tree but a three-story house! It was an old-fashioned mansion, complete with a tower-attic, built to order for a bat!

Weeks went by and finally there was a dress rehearsal. Hattie watched in amazement as an actor wearing a long black cape and looking like an enormous bat began to climb in and out of the windows of the house.

"Why doesn't he fly the way I do?" she said to herself. "I could show that actor how to act like a bat." But Hattie didn't dare move from her perch.

Now at last, it was opening night.

Everybody backstage was nervous and excited, but Mr. Collins was more nervous than anyone else. He was worried about Hattie. She had indeed been very good, but would she still stay out of sight on this, the most important night of all?

Outside the theatre, people in elegant evening clothes were beginning to arrive.

They settled into their seats and began reading the programs. Since they had come to see a mystery play, they were ready and eager to be scared out of their wits.

The auditorium lights dimmed and everyone was silent. Slowly the curtain went up.
The actor dressed as a bat entered and tiptoed across the stage.

The audience groaned. They had seen plays about bat-men many times before.
Several people began to yawn.

"I wanted to see a *scary* play," said one lady, sighing.

"So did I," whispered another. "Bat-men! How boring!"

But there was one small creature in the theater who was not bored.

High in the rafters, Hattie was enchanted by the glorious blue light that flooded
the stage. "A perfect night for a bat like me!" thought Hattie. She could hold herself
back no longer!

Spreading her wings wide, down she flew, sweeping through the open attic
window . . .

swooping across the beam of the bright spotlight above the heads of the audience.
As Hattie darted and wheeled in the shaft of light, suddenly something terrifying
appeared to the audience!

She cast a gigantic shadow across the entire stage!

Men gasped! Ladies screamed! Eyes popped and hair stood on end.
Everyone was scared stiff.

What a commotion! The audience became hysterical when they realized that it was a
real bat swerving and soaring above their heads.

The uproar was too much for Hattie. All at once, in plain sight of everybody, she flew
back through the attic window and disappeared backstage.

The audience stood and cheered. "Bravo, bat!" they shouted. "Bravo!" Hattie had indeed saved the show. To the delight of all the actors, the play was a smashing success.

Of course, Hattie was asked to perform her dazzling flying act each night thereafter. She was a sensational star, and as you might expect, every night after every show Mr. Collins proudly presented to Hattie

a delicious white rose.